Notes for parents

The story has been written in a special way to help young children succeed in their first efforts to read.

Read the whole story aloud first, talking about the pictures as you go. Then encourage your child to read the short, simpler text at the top of each page and read the longer text underneath the pictures yourself. Taking turns with reading builds confidence and children do love joining in.

You can also help your child learn to recognize the important words from this story by looking at the inside back cover where each word is shown next to its picture.

This delightful book provides an enjoyable way for parents and children to share the excitement of learning to read.

Managing designer: **Mary Cartwright** • Photographic manipulation: **John Russell**
Additional models: **Stefan Barnett**, **Les Pickstock**, **Barry Jones**, **Steven Lumley** and **Non Figg**

USBORNE EASY READING

The Missing Cat

Felicity Brooks

Models by Jo Litchfield Designed by Non Figg

Language consultant: Dr. Marlynne Grant Bsc, CertEd, MEdPsych, PhD, AFBPs, CPsychol

Photography by Howard Allman Edited by Jenny Tyler

This story is about Polly and Jack Dot.

Here they are with Mr. Dot, Mrs. Dot and Pip the dog.

This is Littletown where they all live.

There is a little blue bird to find on every page

TED SMART

First published in 1999 by Usborne Publishing Ltd. Usborne House, 83-85 Saffron Hill, London EC1N 8RT, England. www.usborne.com Copyright © 1999 Usborne Publishing Ltd. The name Usborne and the device ⊕ are Trade Marks of Usborne Publishing Ltd. All rights reserved. No part of this publication may be reproduced, stored in a retrieval system, or transmitted in any form or by any means electronic, mechanical, photocopying, recording or otherwise, without prior permission of the publisher. UE Printed in Italy.
This edition produced for:
The Book People Ltd, Hall Wood Avenue, Haydock, St Helens WA11 9UL

Polly, Jack and Mrs. Dot are out shopping.

They are going to the butcher's shop to buy Pip a bone.

Mrs. Beef, the butcher, looks sad.

"My black cat, Oscar, is missing," she says.
"I'm going out to look for him."

"Can we look for Oscar too?" asks Polly.

"Just for a short while," says Mrs. Dot.

They ask the postman. He hasn't seen a black cat.

They ask at the grocer's. "There's no black cat here."

They ask at the market. "There's no black cat here."

"Let's ask at the pet shop," says Polly.

But there's no one there to ask. "There's no black cat in there," says Jack. "Let's try the café."

They ask at the café.

"There are no black cats here."

"Look at these paw prints!" says Polly.

"Maybe Oscar made them," says Jack.
"Let's see where they go."

The paw prints go into the baker's shop.

"They are Pip's paw prints, not Oscar's," says Polly.
"Bad dog!" says Mrs. Dot.

Polly sees a black cat.

"Look," she says. "There's Oscar."
"He can't get down from the roof," says Jack.

Just then the fire truck comes by.

"Can I help?" asks Mr. Sparks, the fireman.
Polly points at the black cat. "Please rescue Oscar."

Mr. Sparks props up his ladder.

He climbs up the ladder.
"I'll save him," he says.

"Come on, Oscar. Don't
be frightened."

He carries the cat down
the ladder.

"Thank you," says Jack.
"Mrs. Beef will be pleased."

They take the cat to the butcher's shop.

But the shop is closed. "Mrs. Beef might be at home,"
says Mrs. Dot. "Let's go and see."

"Hello, Mrs. Beef. Here's Oscar," says Jack.

"That's not Oscar," says Mrs. Beef.

"This is Oscar. He was here when I came home."

"So who does *this* black cat belong to?" says Jack.

"I've no idea. It should go back where you found it."

Just then the cat jumps out of Jack's arms.

"You've found Missy!" cries Mrs. Bird from the pet shop.
"Thank you. I've been looking for her all day."

"Come and see Missy's new kittens."

Mrs. Bird leads the way to the pet shop. "We've seen lots of cats today," says Polly. "But I like dogs best," says Jack.

Here are some of Littletown's cats.

a fat cat,

a thin cat,

a lazy cat,

a big cat,

a tiny cat,

a striped cat,

a fluffy cat,

a smelly cat

and a grumpy cat.

Can you find them all?

The words in *Usborne Easy Reading* books have been carefully chosen and often repeated to help develop your child's early reading skills. Here are some of the important words you will find in *The Missing Cat:*

Polly

Jack

Mrs. Dot

shops

Pip

Mrs. Beef

black

cat

paw print

fire truck

fireman

ladder

Mrs. Bird

With thanks to **Eberhard Faber** for providing the **Fimo**® material for models and also to the **Model shop**, 151 City Road, London.